A Beginning-to-Read Book

Four Good Friends

by Margaret Hillert

Illustrated by Krystyna Stasiak

NORWOOD HOUSE PRESS

DEAR CAREGIVER,

The *Beginning-to-Read* series is a carefully written collection of classic readers you may remember from your own childhood. Each book features text comprised of common sight words to provide your child ample practice reading the words that appear most frequently in written text. The many additional details in the pictures enhance the story and offer the opportunity for you to help your child expand oral language and develop comprehension.

Begin by reading the story to your child, followed by letting him or her read familiar words and soon your child will be able to read the story independently. At each step of the way, be sure to praise your reader's efforts to build his or her confidence as an independent reader. Discuss the pictures and encourage your child to make connections between the story and his or her own life. At the end of the story, you will find reading activities and a word list that will help your child practice and strengthen beginning reading skills.

Above all, the most important part of the reading experience is to have fun and enjoy it!

Shannon Cannon

Shannon Cannon,
Literacy Consultant

Norwood House Press • P.O. Box 316598 • Chicago, Illinois 60631
For more information about Norwood House Press please visit our website at
www.norwoodhousepress.com or call 866-565-2900.

LIBRARY OF CONGRESS CATALOGING-IN-PUBLICATION DATA

Hillert, Margaret.
   Four good friends : the Bremen town musicians retold / by Margaret Hillert;
   illustrated by Krystyna Stasiak. — Rev. and expanded library ed.
     p. cm. — (Beginning-to-read book)
   Summary: A retelling of the Grimm fairy tale in which four animal friends,
   in search of a place to live, scare robbers from a house in the forest and
   decide to live together. Includes reading activities.
   ISBN-13: 978-1-59953-047-5 (library binding : alk. paper)
   ISBN-10: 1-59953-047-3 (library binding : alk. paper)
   [1. Fairy tales. 2. Folklore—Germany.] I. Stasiak, Krystyna, ill. II.
Bremen town musicians. English. III. Title. IV. Series: Hillert, Margaret.
Beginning to read series. Fairy tales and folklore.
   PZ8.H5425Fo 2007
   398.2—dc22
   [E]   2006007893

I can not work.
No one wants me.
I have to go away.
Away, away, away.

Oh, my. Oh, my.
You do not look good, little one.
Why?
What is it?

I can not work.
No one wants me.
I am no good.

Come. Come.
I like you.
You can come with me.

See here now.
We will go away.
We will find something.

What is this?
What have we here?
You are a big one.

I can not run.
I can not work.
What will I do now?
Where will I go?

You are big.
Big, big, big.
You can help us.

You can come with us.
We want you.
Come with us to see
what we can find.

My, how pretty you are.
But, what is it?
Can we help?

I am no good, I guess.
No one wants me.
What am I to do?

Do you want to come with us?
We like you.
We want you.

Look here.
A little house.
Is this what we want?

Have a look.
What do you see?
What is in this house?

I see a man.
I see two.
I see three.

We want to see, too.
Do it like this.
Here we go.
Up and up and up.

Oh, oh, oh!
Oh, my. Oh, my!
Oh, look at that!

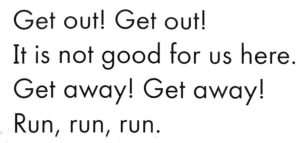

Get out! Get out!
It is not good for us here.
Get away! Get away!
Run, run, run.

Now that is funny.
What did we do?
But come in here.
It looks good in here.

Now we have a house.
We have something to eat.
We do not have to work.
We are happy.

The following activities support the findings of the National Reading Panel that determined the most effective components for reading instruction are: Phonemic Awareness, Phonics, Vocabulary, Fluency, and Text Comprehension.

Phonemic Awareness: The /f/ sound

Oral Blending: Say the beginning sounds listed below and ask your child to say the word formed by adding the /**f**/ sound to the end:

roo + /f/ = roof	lea + /f/ = leaf	che + /f/ = chef
hu + /f/ = huff	li + /f/ = life	wol + /f/ = wolf
loa + /f/ = loaf	bee + /f/ = beef	el + /f/ = elf
shel + /f/ = shelf	kni + /f/ = knife	scar + /f/ = scarf

Phonics: The letter Ff

1. Demonstrate how to form the letters **F** and **f** for your child.
2. Have your child practice writing **F** and **f** at least three times each.
3. Ask your child to point to the words in the book that begin with the letter **f**.
4. Write down the following words and ask your child to circle the letter **f** in each word:

for	fun	raft	fur	foot
fast	roof	if	sift	friend
fold	lift	fluff	flat	stuff

Vocabulary: Synonyms

1. Write the following words on separate pieces of paper:

small	scared	house	thin	joyful
big	slender	nice	happy	afraid
little	excellent	tired	run	make
sleepy	jog	large	create	pretty
good	home	lovely	great	

2. Read each word to your child and ask your child to repeat it.

3. Explain to your child that when two different words mean almost the same thing, they are called synonyms.

4. Mix the words up. Point to a word and ask your child to read it. Provide clues if your child needs them. Ask your child to match the pairs of synonym words.

Fluency: Shared Reading

1. Reread the story to your child at least two more times while your child tracks the print by running a finger under the words as they are read. Ask your child to read the words he or she knows with you.

2. Reread the story taking turns, alternating readers between sentences or pages.

Text Comprehension: Discussion Time

1. Ask your child to retell the sequence of events in the story.

2. To check comprehension, ask your child the following questions:

   • Why did the animals think no one wanted them?

   • How did the animals help each other?

   • Why did the men leave the house?

   • Could this story really happen? Why or why not?

   • Can you describe a time when you felt bad but everything turned out okay?

WORD LIST

Four Good Friends uses the 61 words listed below.
This list can be used to practice reading the words that appear in the text. You may wish to write the words on index cards and use them to help your child build automatic word recognition. Regular practice with these words will enhance your child's fluency in reading connected text.

a	get	man	that
am	go	me	this
and	good	my	three
away	guess		to
		no	too
big	happy	not	two
but	have	now	
	help		up
can	here	oh	us
come	house	one	
	how	out	want(s)
did			we
do	I	pretty	what
	in		where
eat	is	run	why
	it		will
find		see	with
for	like	something	work
funny	little		
	look(s)		you

ABOUT THE AUTHOR Margaret Hillert has written over 80 books for children who are just learning to read. Her books have been translated into many different languages and over a million children throughout the world have read her books. She first started writing poetry as a child and has continued to write for children and adults throughout her life. A first grade teacher for 34 years, Margaret is now retired from teaching and lives in Michigan where she likes to write, take walks in the morning, and care for her three cats.

Photograph by Glenna Washburn

ABOUT THE ADVISER Shannon Cannon contributed the activities pages that appear in this book. Shannon serves as a literacy consultant and provides staff development to help improve reading instruction. She is a frequent presenter at educational conferences and workshops. Prior to this she worked as an elementary school teacher and as president of a curriculum publishing company.